How Brown Mouse Kept Christmas

•

Clyde Watson

Pictures by

Wendy Watson

Farrar Straus Giroux
New York

Text copyright © 1980 by Clyde Watson
Pictures copyright © 1980 by Wendy Watson
All rights reserved
Published simultaneously in Canada by
McGraw-Hill Ryerson Ltd., Toronto
Printed in the United States of America by Eastern Press
Color separations by Offset Separations Corp.
Bound by A. Horowitz and Sons
Designed by Nanette Stevenson
First edition, 1980
Library of Congress Cataloging in Publication Data
Watson, Clyde. How brown mouse kept Christmas.
[1. Christmas stories. 2. Mice—Fiction]
I. Watson, Wendy. II. Title.
PZ7.W3263Ho   1980   [E]   80-18532
ISBN 0-374-33494-3

7005685

To Mary Cameron

for whom this story was specially made up
when it was time for bed on Christmas Eve
and just beginning to snow

It was Christmas Eve, and in the big house the children ran around in bare feet and nighties, hanging up their stockings for Santa Claus. The grownups stood on chairs to tie doves and angels on the highest branches of the tree, and outside, soft snowflakes were falling thick and slow.

Someone lit the candles, and Aunt Kate played carols on the piano while everybody sang; but then the children had to be tucked into bed for the night.

Some lay awake for a time, and in the stillness of the house they listened to the curious, peaceful sound of mice scampering in the attic. From downstairs came faint clinks and laughter: the grownups were washing up the dishes—but soon they went to bed too, and the snow kept falling thicker and deeper.

Up in the attic, the mice were wide awake. They know all about Christmastime, when the pantry is full of cakes and fruit and spilled sugar. They had been teasing the cat all day, trying to tire her out so when nighttime came she'd lie down on the hearth and fall into deep sleep.

There was one quite small mouse, named Brown Mouse, who had never been down in the people part of the house, he was that young. But he had certainly heard of Christmas, and he wanted to go and see it with the rest.

"Well, Brown Mouse," said the other mice, "you're pretty small to go down there—what if the cat woke up and saw you?"

But Brown Mouse pestered and bothered around until finally the oldest mouse said, "All right, Brown Mouse: if you come with us carefully and do what we do, then when the people are asleep and the cat is too, and the big clock in the hall strikes twelve, we will take you downstairs and out the mousehole."

Brown Mouse was patient, and at last the big clock in the hall struck twelve, and then it was time. So under the floor and over the wires, through the walls and along the pipes went the oldest mouse and Brown Mouse and the other mice too. They went out the mousehole in the pantry, across the kitchen floor, into the living room, and there! what a sight they saw:

A tall, tall tree
all spicy and green
hung with hundreds of
twinkling, glittering
things of all sorts:
red, blue and gold glass balls
and bells and Santas;
apples, stars, paper chains,
tiny packages dangling from threads
and silvery light
trembling on every branch,
casting crisscross shadows
on the ceiling . . .

The cat lay dreaming by the red coals of the fire, and snowflakes pecked the window outside as they kept on falling deep and white.

The mice ran in and out among the packages under the tree, up and down the branches, tasting things and looking. There was no end of good things to eat—not just everyday crumbs, mind you, but whole lovely cookies and nuts and raisins. Besides that, there were treasures that even the smallest mouse could carry: tinsel ribbons and red beads and scraps of soft stuff for nests...

The other mice knew just what they wanted, but Brown Mouse was so astonished he didn't know where to begin, so he scampered all over the room, sniffing and nibbling and exploring.

He scurried up onto the piano and ate a candied cherry that was left there on a plate; and then he ran down inside the piano to look for more, and his little mouse feet on the strings made faint, tingly music.

Up on the mantelpiece, he played in the quivering tangle of light and shadows from the tree, and he darted in among the branches and tasted sugarplums and ginger elves. At the bottom of the tree he met a doll, who smiled and stared at him with green glass eyes.

He even found a tiny gold hoop down in a crack by the hearth, a wonderful Christmas toy that rolled and spun and sparkled as he chased it— but when the cat mumbled in her sleep, Brown Mouse dropped the hoop and ran away.

All night long, the snow sifted down and piled in drifts outside the windows of the house, while the mice made trips in and out the mousehole, back and forth from the Christmas tree to their home in the attic, taking bits of things with them as they went.

And they didn't think it strange at all when an old, white-haired man came down the chimney in the middle of the night and tiptoed around for a while, putting secrets into stockings and talking to the cat.

When the big clock in the hall struck five, the night was nearly over and it was time for the mice to leave.

"We have to go now, Brown Mouse," said the oldest mouse, "so pick something special to bring with you"—for Brown Mouse had been so busy all night that he hadn't carried a single thing up to the attic!

"Hurry up," whispered the other mice. "Take something and come on!"

So Brown Mouse nipped up a piece of tinsel and headed for the mousehole with the rest of the mice—but when they reached the kitchen door he turned around, and paused there on the sill, looking back at the Christmas tree with its shimmering lights and lacy shadows, and the doll with the green glass eyes, and the cat sleeping on the hearth—

And then he squeaked and whisked across the floor to catch up with the other mice, for he didn't want to be the last one through the mousehole.

By Christmas morning the snow had stopped and the world was brilliant in the sun. The cat woke up and stretched, and when the children came down to the Christmas tree, everything looked perfect and they just stared.

But when they started looking closer, they did notice a few odd details: one of the ginger elves had its boots nibbled off, and there were crumbs on the sofa; there was tinsel out in the kitchen, and the top of the coffee cake was missing a cherry or two.

Most strange of all, there on the hearth lay Mother's wedding ring, which had been lost for months.

"Now how do you explain that?" they all wondered—but nobody knew.

After breakfast, the children went outdoors to try their Christmas sleds on the new snow, and the cat sat on the window ledge washing her fur. And up in the attic, tired after a long night of feasting and merrymaking, a small brown mouse was fast asleep, with sugar on his whiskers.

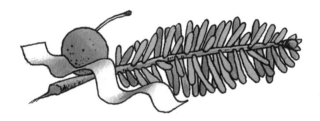